This edition published by Parragon Books Ltd in 2015

Parragon Books Ltd
Chartist House
15–17 Trim Street
Bath BA1 1HA, UK
www.parragon.com

ISBN 978-1-4748-0302-1

Printed in China

Anna's
Book of Secrets

PaRragon

Bath • New York • Singapore • Hong Kong • Cologne • Delhi
Melbourne • Amsterdam • Johannesburg • Shenzhen

From the movie
DISNEY
FROZEN

THIS BOOK BELONGS TO

Arrianna xxx

The kingdom of Arendelle was a busy and happy place, nestled high among the mountains of the far north. At night, the colourful Northern Lights often lit up the sky in beautiful patterns.

A kind king and queen ruled Arendelle. Their young daughters, Elsa and Anna, were the joy of their lives. But the royal couple had a secret worry....

Their eldest daughter, Elsa,
had a magical power. She could
create snow and freeze things with just
one touch!

Anna, the younger daughter,
adored her big sister and the two
were always together. One night, Anna and
Elsa sneaked into the Great Hall in the castle and
created a winter wonderland!

But while the girls were playing Elsa accidentally hit
Anna with a blast of icy magic. Little Anna fell to the
ground, shivering. A streak of white appeared in her hair.
Frightened for her sister, Elsa called out for help.

The worried king and queen rushed their daughters
to the realm of trolls – the trolls were mysterious healers
who knew about magic.

A wise old troll explained that Anna could be cured, but he also had a warning about Elsa's power. "There is beauty in it but also great danger," he said. "She must learn to control it."

The worried king and queen taught Elsa to hide her power. But whenever she had strong feelings the magic spilled out. So the king gave her a pair of gloves to hold it back.

The troll also changed little Anna's memories so that she wouldn't remember Elsa's power.

Elsa decided that to keep Anna safe, it would be best to stay away from her.

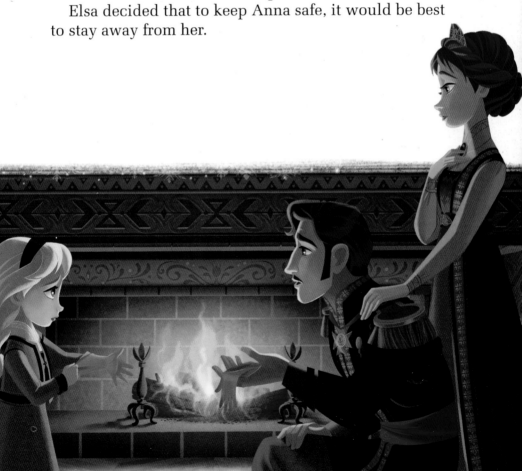

As the girls grew, Anna kept trying to spend time with her sister. But Elsa always said that she was busy – she was afraid that she might hurt Anna again.

As the years passed the girls became more and more like strangers. Then, when the two were teenagers, the king and queen were tragically lost in a storm at sea. The sisters felt sadder and more alone than ever.

When Elsa was old enough, she became queen.
Guests from far away sailed into Arendelle for
the coronation.

Anna was excited to meet so many people –
especially a handsome young prince called Hans!

Meanwhile, Elsa was still struggling to hide her powers. She just hoped that she could make it through the day without anybody finding out about them.

 To Elsa's relief the celebration went exactly as planned.
Everybody cheered for their beautiful new queen.
 Afterwards, a party was held in the Great Hall. Anna and
Prince Hans spent the evening laughing, dancing and talking.
They had so much in common! Everything seemed perfect,
so they made a big decision....

Anna introduced Hans to Elsa –
and announced that they were going
to be married.

Elsa was shocked. "You can't
marry a man you've just met,"
she told Anna.

Elsa started to leave the room,
but Anna grabbed her hand and
accidentally pulled off her
sister's glove!

Anna was confused and angry.
"Why do you shut me out?" she asked.
"I can't live like this anymore!"

"Enough!" Elsa cried. An icy blast shot from her ungloved hand sending a sheet of ice across the ballroom! Everyone stared in disbelief.

Elsa fled the castle, worried that her secret had finally been revealed and terrified that she might hurt someone.

"Stay away from me!" she warned the townspeople as she hurried past them.

Everything around Elsa turned to ice as she ran. She stepped on to the fjord and the water froze solid! Ships at the harbour became locked in the ice as she raced towards the mountains in the distance.

Elsa climbed up into the mountains and with nobody around to worry about, she let all her power loose for the first time. She felt free! A blizzard whirled around her. She even turned her own dress into a beautiful icy gown.

As she neared the top of the mountain, Elsa created a magnificent, shining ice palace. At last she felt like the person she was always meant to be!

Elsa's blizzard had covered Arendelle with snow. Anna knew that she had to find Elsa to thaw out the land – plus, she wanted her big sister back. Now that Elsa's secret was out, they could finally be close again!

Leaving Hans in charge of the kingdom, Anna rode into the mountains. The storm made the journey difficult, though, especially when Anna's horse threw her into the snow. Luckily, she spotted a small building up ahead.

The building was a shop for travellers. Anna rushed
in and immediately gathered up some supplies.

A young man named Kristoff was also collecting winter
supplies. He mentioned that a storm was coming down
from the North Mountain.

Anna began asking questions. If the storm was on the
North Mountain, Elsa would be there, too!

But Kristoff was busy bargaining for supplies.
Feeling crowded, he blurted out, "Now back up, while
I deal with this crook!"

The insulted shopkeeper threw him out of his shop!

This gave Anna an idea.
She found Kristoff in the stable,
where he was singing to his beloved
reindeer, Sven. She offered to give him the
supplies he needed if he took her to find Elsa.
Finally, Kristoff agreed. "We leave at dawn."
"No," said Anna. "We leave right now."

Anna and Kristoff climbed on
to a sledge and Sven began
pulling them up the mountain.

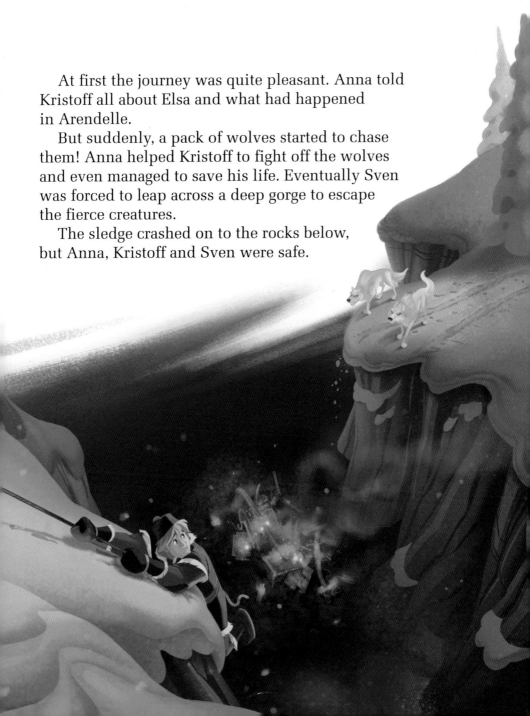

At first the journey was quite pleasant. Anna told
Kristoff all about Elsa and what had happened
in Arendelle.

But suddenly, a pack of wolves started to chase
them! Anna helped Kristoff to fight off the wolves
and even managed to save his life. Eventually Sven
was forced to leap across a deep gorge to escape
the fierce creatures.

The sledge crashed on to the rocks below,
but Anna, Kristoff and Sven were safe.

The trio continued into the forest on foot. They soon
came across a beautiful winter scene. Anna was more
eager than ever to find Elsa – she had to know more about
her sister's amazing power!

"I never knew winter could be so ... beautiful,"
Anna said.

"But it's so white," added a voice. "How about some colour?"

It was a living snowman!

"I'm Olaf," he said, explaining that Elsa had made him.

Anna asked Olaf to lead them to her sister. "We need Elsa to bring back summer."

Olaf grinned. "I've always loved the idea of summer," he said. "The warm sun on my face, getting a gorgeous tan. Just doing whatever snow does in summer."

But Anna and Kristoff were thinking the same thing: summer would not be good for a snowman!

The path up the mountain grew more and more difficult. Luckily, Olaf soon found a stairway made of ice leading straight to Elsa's palace.

"Whoa," exclaimed Anna in awe as they reached the top. The ice palace was amazing!

They approached the front door and Anna knocked. After a moment, the door swung open.

Elsa was worried to see Anna. She wanted to return home with her sister, but she knew that everything would be different now that her secret was out. She also remembered how dangerous her powers could be.

"I think you should go, Anna," Elsa said. "I'm sorry.
It has to be this way."

But Anna explained that Arendelle was still frozen. If Elsa
stayed away, everyone in the kingdom would freeze to death!

Now Elsa was scared. She admitted to Anna that she didn't know how to undo her magic.

Anna was sure that they could work it out together, but Elsa thought that was impossible. It crushed her to know she was still a danger to others.

Elsa's feelings overwhelmed her until her powers burst
out of her – and struck her sister in the heart!

Anna refused to leave, feeling certain that she could
still help her sister. But Elsa insisted – and conjured up
a giant snowman to escort Anna outside, along with
Kristoff and Olaf.

"Hey, you made me a little brother," Olaf said to Elsa happily. He turned to the huge snowman. "I'm going to name you Marshmallow!"

Elsa ordered Marshmallow to escort Anna and her companions off the mountain. But after Anna hit him with a snowball, he decided to chase them, instead!

The friends ran until they reached a cliff and then lowered themselves down the side. But Marshmallow grabbed the rope and pulled them back up. Anna did the only thing she could think of – she cut the rope!

Luckily, Anna, Kristoff and Olaf landed safely in a soft snowdrift down below. But something was wrong with Anna – her hair was turning white!

"What happened back there? What did she do to you?" Kristoff asked.

Anna explained that Elsa had struck her with her powers.
Kristoff knew just what to do. He had some friends who
were experts at just about everything. They could help Anna!

Night fell as Kristoff led Anna and Olaf to the secret realm of the trolls. Seeing Kristoff, the trolls came out of hiding. He had spent a lot of time with them as he was growing up, so he was practically family!

When an old troll touched Anna's hair, he understood immediately that she had been hurt.

One of the trolls explained that Elsa's magic had struck ice into Anna's heart, which would cause her to freeze solid by tomorrow! But there was still hope. "An act of true love can thaw a frozen heart," the troll said.

Thinking quickly, Olaf and Kristoff decided to take Anna back home. Surely her true love, Prince Hans, could break the spell with a true love's kiss.

Back in Arendelle Hans had become worried when Anna's horse had returned without her. So he had gathered volunteers to help him find Anna and capture Elsa.

When Hans's group arrived at the ice palace Elsa had tried to protect herself. But in the struggle she was hit by falling ice. She was taken back to Arendelle as a prisoner.

Kristoff and Anna had no idea what had happened at Elsa's ice palace. Kristoff took Anna to the castle gates at Arendelle and sadly passed her over to the servants.

He was starting to realize that he cared deeply about Anna. But he knew she was in grave danger ... and that her true love, Hans, would be able to make her well again.

The servants built a fire in the library to warm Anna, but she was still getting colder by the minute.

Anna was so glad when Hans arrived. She explained what Elsa's icy blast had done and how his kiss could cure her. "Only an act of true love can save me," she said.

"Could it be this easy?" Hans asked, his smile turning into a sneer. Then he put out the fire with a jug of water.

Hans explained that he had only been pretending to be in love with her so that he could rule Arendelle!

With Anna nearly frozen, Hans saw that his dream was within reach. All he had to do now was to get rid of Elsa.

"You can't," Anna gasped. She collapsed to the floor as the ice spread through her body.

Meanwhile, locked in the castle dungeon, all Elsa could think about was getting away from the kingdom to protect everyone from her powers. She was also worried about Anna – but she didn't know that Anna was back in Arendelle, too.

Elsa became so upset that she lost control of her magic again and froze the dungeon. The ice broke her chains and she escaped!

At that same moment, Olaf helped Anna to get to her feet and come outside. The little snowman had realized that Kristoff loved Anna – and that his kiss could save her!

Anna spotted Kristoff running over to her and she began to move slowly towards him, almost completely frozen. But then she saw something else – Hans was about to strike Elsa with his sword!

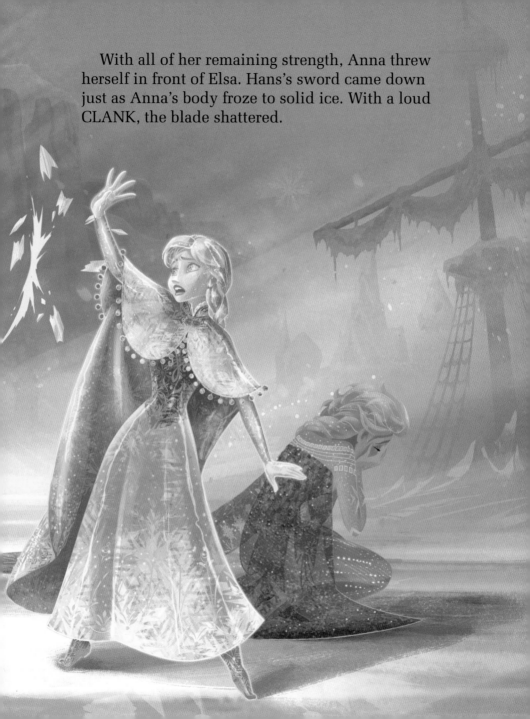

With all of her remaining strength, Anna threw herself in front of Elsa. Hans's sword came down just as Anna's body froze to solid ice. With a loud CLANK, the blade shattered.

Elsa wept as she wrapped her arms around her sister. "Oh, Anna," she sobbed.

A moment passed. Then something amazing happened. Anna began to thaw! "Elsa?" she whispered.

"You sacrificed yourself for me?" Elsa asked. Anna nodded weakly.

"An act of true love will thaw a frozen heart," Olaf said.

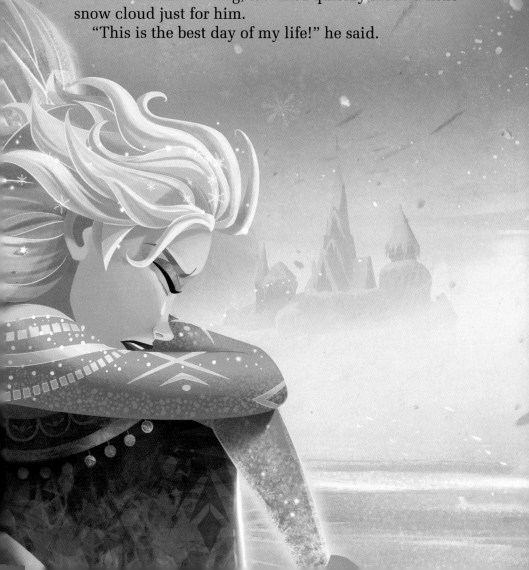

With her sacrifice, Anna had helped Elsa to see that love was more powerful than fear.

Suddenly, Elsa realized that love was the force that could control her powers. She raised her arms and the ice and snow that covered Arendelle melted away.

But Olaf was melting, too! Elsa quickly made a little snow cloud just for him.

"This is the best day of my life!" he said.

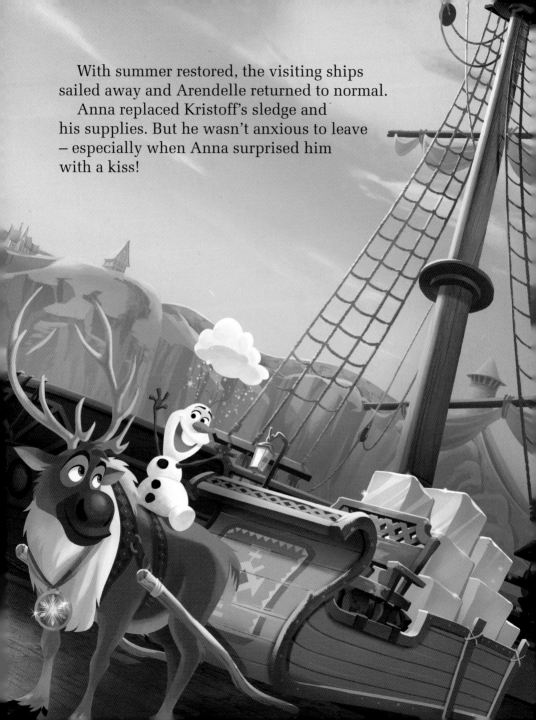

With summer restored, the visiting ships
sailed away and Arendelle returned to normal.
Anna replaced Kristoff's sledge and
his supplies. But he wasn't anxious to leave
– especially when Anna surprised him
with a kiss!

Elsa created
an ice-skating rink in
the castle and threw open the
gates of the kingdom – she never planned to
close them again.

Everyone had a
wonderful time skating
with Queen Elsa and
Princess Anna. The kingdom of
Arendelle was a happy place
once more!

From the movie
Disney
FROZEN

All About Me

Anna wants to know everything about you! Write down all your details on these pages so you can keep them between you and Anna.

Name...

Nickname...

Birthday..

Hair colour..

Eye colour..

Address...

....

....

....

Email..

Phone..

Best friend...

Pets..

....

Family..

....

....

My best talent...

....

My worst habit..

....

My happiest memory..

....

....

Thing I am most proud of..................................

....

....

Secret Gallery

Create your very own special gallery of ... you! Stick photos of yourself on these pages and keep them secretly stashed away.

Stick a photo of yourself here!

Me as a baby

Me on holiday

Me at home

Family Forever

Family is very important to Anna, especially when she realizes that she has a lot to learn about her sister. Make sure you find out all there is to know about your family and write it down on these pages.

Who makes you laugh the most?..

Who is best at helping you out?..

Who makes the most mess?..

Who gives the best hugs?..

How do your family describe you?

....

....

....

....

Stick your favourite family photograph here!

Sweet Dreams

Anna dreams of making new friends.
What do you dream about? Keep your
own secret dream diary!

Rate your dream

😊 for fun

😫 for scary

😆 for fun + scary!

Date ....
What my dream was about...
....
....
Rating ....

Date ....
What my dream was about...
....
....
Rating ....

Date ....
What my dream was about...
....
....
Rating ....

Date ....
What my dream was about...
....
....
Rating ....

Date ....
What my dream was about...
....
....
Rating ....

Amazing Adventures

Anna, Kristoff, Sven and Olaf set off on a chilly adventure to find Elsa. Would you like to go on an amazing trip? Write about it here!

Where would you go?...

....

When would you go?...

....

How long would you go for?...

....

Who would you go with?...

....

....

....

....

Stuff to pack ....
....
....
....

Stuff to see ....
....
....
....

Stuff to do ....
....
....
....

Magical Memories!

Anna cherishes her memories of playing with her sister when she was little. Keep hold of your most treasured memories by creating a box filled with secrets and moments to remember.

How to make your memory box:

Grab a box – even an old shoebox will do! Fill it with things that you treasure and want to remember always. Then tuck it away in a safe place. Many years from now, you'll be glad you kept those things!

What is your first memory?

Arrianna Karis
y

I

Which item do you treasure the most and why?

Friends Lowdown

How well do you know your friends?
Fill in these details about your best
friends, then ask them for their answers
to see how well you did!

Stick their
picture here!

Name
....

What is their favourite movie?
....

Who makes them laugh the most?
....

What is their dream?
....
....
....

Stick their
picture here!

Name

....

What is their favourite movie?

....

Who makes them laugh the most?

....

What is their dream?

....

....

....

Stick their picture here!

Name
....
What is their favourite movie?
....
Who makes them laugh the most?
....
What is their dream?
....
....
....

Stick their
picture here!

Name

....

What is their favourite movie?

....

Who makes them laugh the most?

....

What is their dream?

....

....

....

Sister Secrets

Anna's sister has been keeping a very big secret from her. Can you keep secrets too? Write about them here.

What's the biggest secret you've ever shared?

ArrAYTAY

on a ° B

Rরi০Fার pর

HৰRp

Have you ever shared someone else's secret? What was it?

Which secrets would you share with Anna?

Attiann or Ri'ov

WRA

What's the funniest secret you've ever heard?

Sparkling Birthdays

To help you remember the most important day of the year for your friends and family you can write everyone's birthdays here. Think of some amazing gift ideas for each birthday, too!

Name *Brooke* ....
Birthday *Junvle* ....
Age this year ....
Gift ideas ....

....

Name ....
Birthday ....
Age this year ....
Gift ideas ....

....

Name ....

Birthday ....

Age this year ....

Gift ideas ....

....

Name ....

Birthday ....

Age this year ....

Gift ideas ....

....

Name ....

Birthday ....

Age this year ....

Gift ideas ....

....

Perfect Princess

Anna is the Princess of Arendelle – she lives in a majestic castle and wears beautiful dresses. If you were a princess what would you do every day, and what would you like to wear?

Princess name ....

Princess duties ....

....

If I were a princess I would ....

....

....

Describe your favourite royal dress!

....

....

....

....

Draw your perfect princess dress here!

Summer Fun And Snowy Hugs

Anna's snowy friend Olaf wants to hang out in the summer time and get warm hugs. What kind of things do you like to do with your friends in the summer? Fill in your wishes here.

....

....

....

....

....

....

....

Rate these things from 1–10.
(1 is your least favourite and 10 is your most favourite).

☑ Hanging out with friends

☑ Hanging out with family

☑ Winter time

☑ Summer time

☑ Going to school

☑ Doing homework

☑ Going to a sleepover party

☑ Daydreaming

☑ Cleaning my room

☑ Making a snowman

Animal Friends

Sven is a comical reindeer and becomes one of Anna's closest friends. Do you have any animal friends? If you don't, fill in these pages for your dream pet.

Type of animal

....

Name BROOKe

....

Age

....

Colour

....

Favourite food

....

Favourite game

....

Best trick

....

I love my animal friend because

....

....

....

....

Stick a photo of your animal friend here!

Summer Celebration

Anna wants to throw Olaf a summer-themed party so he can enjoy summer fun, but without the heat! Help her plan the party and write your ideas here.

Sunny-style drinks

1. ....
2. RRAOMOVN O
3. ....

Picnic snacks

1. ....
2. ....
3. ....

Summer songs to sing

1. ....
2. ....
3. ....

Tropical party games

1 ...... *omgm* ....

2 ....

3 ....

How would you decorate your party?
Draw your idea for Olaf's party below.